Disney
FAIRIES

TinkerBell
AND THE
PirateFairy

PaRragon

Bath • New York • Cologne • Melbourne • Delhi
Hong Kong • Shenzhen • Singapore • Amsterdam

One beautiful day in Pixie Hollow, Rosetta, Silvermist and Iridessa were planting sunflowers when Zarina walked past. "Hey, Zarina! Out of pixie dust again?" asked Rosetta. Fairies use pixie dust to fly, but Zarina preferred to walk. "Just out for a stroll. You know me!" Zarina said.

Zarina was a dust-keeper fairy and, one day, it was her turn to pour the special Blue Pixie Dust into the Pixie Dust Tree.

The Blue Pixie Dust was powerful – mixing it with golden pixie dust made the gold dust multiply!

Zarina asked Fairy Gary, the head dust-keeper, if they could make other colours of pixie dust. Fairy Gary warned her, "Dust-keepers are forbidden to tamper with pixie dust."

Zarina had secretly been saving up her pixie dust.
After finding a speck of Blue Dust in her hair, Zarina
was inspired to try one of her many failed pixie-dust
experiments again, this time adding a tiny bit of the
Blue Dust speck.

The gold dust turned orange!

Zarina shared her discovery
with her friend Tinker Bell –
the new orange dust allowed
Zarina to bend
a moonbeam!

Zarina wanted to experiment more! But Tink was concerned. "Zarina, I really think you should stop," she said firmly.

Zarina turned and accidentally bumped into a plant, spilling all of her new pink dust on it. The plant's vines grew quickly, bursting out of Zarina's cottage and spreading all over Pixie Hollow. They even crushed the Dust Depot.

Zarina couldn't believe the damage!

When Fairy Gary saw the pink dust, he knew Zarina had been experimenting with pixie dust. He told Zarina she could no longer be a dust-keeper fairy. "You were told not to tamper with pixie dust."

She was devastated. She rushed back home, packed her things and left Pixie Hollow.

One year later, the fairies were celebrating the Four Seasons Festival.

While Periwinkle dazzled the crowd at the amphitheatre with her ice-skating skills, Tink and her friends were backstage working on their act for the show.

As everyone watched Periwinkle's performance, Tinker Bell saw a fairy sprinkling pink dust behind the crowd.

"Wait. Is that ... Zarina?" asked Tink.

Suddenly, flowers sprouted in the amphitheatre – and then they burst open and sprayed pollen into the air. Rosetta knew it would make everyone fall asleep. "Guys! We gotta hide – now!"

After Tink and her friends came out of hiding, they discovered the Blue Pixie Dust was missing!

They followed its blue glow to a rowing boat where they saw Zarina showing the bag of Blue Dust to pirates! Tinker Bell assumed that the pirates had made Zarina take the dust.

But then the fairies watched in shock as a pirate called James said to Zarina, "Let me say, your plan worked perfectly ... *captain*."

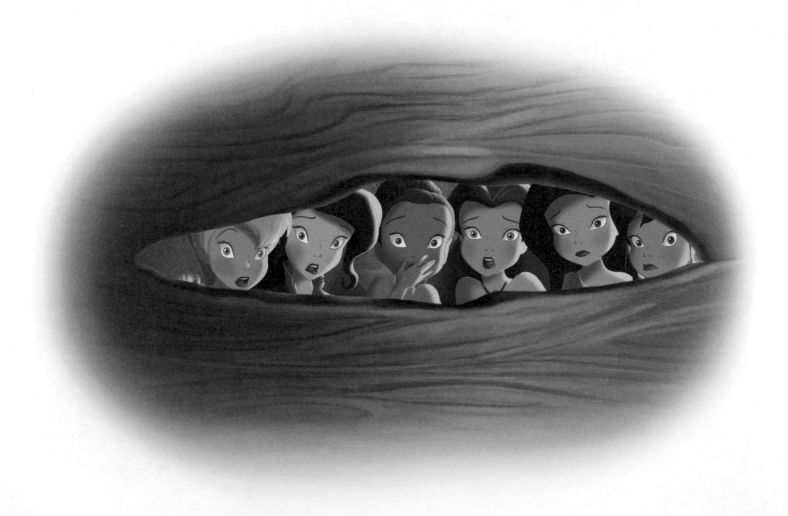

The fairies snatched the bag of
Blue Pixie Dust from the pirates
and flew away from the boat.
"Give me back that dust!"
shouted Zarina as she
chased after them.

Zarina threw multicoloured dust at the fairies, knocking them through a waterfall and out cold. Zarina took back the bag of Blue Pixie Dust and flew off.

When the fairies woke up they discovered that the dust had swapped their talents – and their outfits!

The fairies found the pirate ship that the rowing boat had been taking the Blue Pixie Dust to and they sneaked aboard.

The ship sailed to Skull Rock where, inside, Zarina had grown a Pixie Dust Tree. The pirates wanted the pixie dust from the tree to make their ship fly! Some of the fairies sneaked into Zarina's cabin, where they listened to James and Zarina's plans. The others tried to listen from outside.

James watched Zarina preparing the Blue Pixie Dust. "So the secret is to put the Blue Dust directly into the tree. Very impressive, captain!"

Inside Skull Rock, Zarina and
James made their way to the tree.
Slowly, Zarina tipped a container of
Blue Dust into the dust well of the
tree. Then she saw the fairies.

Zarina drew her sword and called
to her pirate friends, who caught the
fairies in nets.

"Zarina, don't do this! Come back
home," begged Tinker Bell.

"I'll never go back to Pixie Hollow,"
answered Zarina. "This is exactly
where I belong."

Tink and the others were taken to the galley, where the ship's cook put them in an old crab cage. The fairies tried their best to escape, but they were locked up tight.

Meanwhile, Zarina added Blue Pixie Dust to the tree, which started to make golden dust flow. The pirates cheered! Their plan had been a success.

Zarina sprinkled the golden dust on James. She taught him to fly and they soared through the air together. But when they landed back on the ship, James locked Zarina in a lantern. Now that he had the dust, he revealed he had been using her – he had never been her friend.

The fairies finally managed to escape. They did not want Zarina to get hurt, despite her actions. They rushed to help their misguided friend.

Zarina was grateful to Tink and her friends. She apologized and offered to help them catch James.

Zarina led the fairies to the flying ship and they slipped into the captain's cabin undetected – and reappeared looking like swashbucklers!

But the fairies struggled to fight the pirates with their tiny swords.

They realized that if they used their talents together they could defeat the pirates.

Fawn used her new light talent to shoot scorching light-beams down at the pirates.

While Zarina and James fought, the ship started to tip over. James clung to the mast trying not to fall in the sea.

Zarina grabbed the vial of Blue Pixie Dust that he had around his neck. But when he saw the golden pixie dust start to fall from the ship into the sea he reached for it and fell!

James covered himself with golden pixie
dust so that he could fly up and take back the
Blue Dust from Zarina. But one tiny speck of Blue
Dust fell from the vial and Zarina threw it at James.
That made the pixie dust multiply all over James and he flew
wildly – right into the ocean!

The fairies congratulated each other on defeating the pirates and turned the ship round.

Zarina, Tink and the other fairies flew the ship back to Pixie Hollow and Zarina used her dust to wake up everyone in the amphitheatre. Everyone was very happy that Zarina had come back home! The fairies returned the Blue Dust to the vault and Pixie Hollow was saved.